# THE PIGS' BOOK
# OF WORLD RECORDS

by Jovial Bob Stine
pictures by Peter Lippman

Random House 🏠 New York

For Amy and Miss Piggy

*Library of Congress Cataloging in Publication Data:* Stine, Jovial Bob. The pigs' book of world records. SUMMARY: Presents a survey of significant pig achievements, award-winning pigs, pig personalities, examples of pig humor, and other piggish topics.   1. Swine—Anecdotes, facetiae, satire, etc.   2. Wit and humor, Juvenile.   [1. Pigs—Anecdotes, facetiae, satire, etc.   2. Wit and Humor]   I. Lippman, Peter J.   II. Title.   PN6231.S895S74   818'.5'407   79-5239   ISBN: 0-394-84402-5 (trade);   0-394-94402-X (lib. bdg.)

Manufactured in the United States of America     1 2 3 4 5 6 7 8 9 0

Sausage Press, publishers of *Hogwash,*
in association with Porky Publishing Corp.,
creators of porkbound books in hard or soft pork,
in cooperation with The Swill-of-the-Month Club
is proud to present four complete books—
exclusively for pigs—in one fat volume.

# CONTENTS

Other Ingredients: Artificially spoiled bone broth. USDA-approved mon-
odygleric dehydrogenated trough grease (a watery substance that's not
nice to touch), salt, tribenzoate of tribenzoate, artificially over-ripened
slops with vitamin A, seven natural fruit juices, powdered swamp gas (for
added creaminess), unidentified green things with little furry legs, sugar, riboflavin (*everything* has to have riboflavin), monosodiumated chimpanzee
breath, and BHS used as a preservative.

WARNING: The Surgeon General has determined that reading the pre-
vious ingredients list may be hazardous to
your lunch. Please skip it and go on to
the rest of the book.

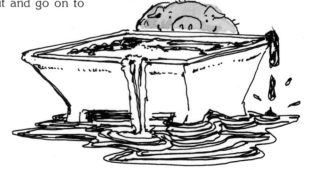

*Also by Jovial Bob Stine*

How To Be Funny
The Absurdly Silly Encyclopedia
and Flyswatter

# BOOK 1

## The Pigs' Book of World Records

With an Introduction
by Abner Doublechin

# INTRODUCTION
## by Abner Doublechin
### (Fairly well-known pig)

I am so pleased to have the honor of introducing this marvelously useful book. Before picking up this volume, I had no idea it was so easy to sew little things onto other little things.

But after reading just one chapter, I was able to sew a buttonhole onto my sister's head. Two chapters later, I was doing fancy embroidery on my uncle. I stitched a lovely plaid tablecloth for the back yard slops trough, as well as a six-foot cloth napkin that almost fits around my chins.

Sewing has never been easy for pigs—especially since it's so hard to sew and eat at the same time. But this book makes it a snap. I believe it will keep you in stitches as well as—

What's that?

Oh my.

I've just been told that I've written my introduction for the wrong book. I thought I was to write an introduction to a book entitled *Swine Stitchery*. But it appears that the book I was supposed to introduce is *The Pigs' Book of World Records*. It's some sort of record book for pigs, I guess.

I don't know much about *that* one, I'm afraid. I've been so busy sewing, I haven't had much time to read.

# World Records

## WORLD'S LARGEST PIG

Mike "Mountain" McPorkenbeans, who once fooled people into thinking he was the state of Delaware, is the largest pig in the world. McPorkenbeans is so large, no one has ever dared tell him he's a pig!

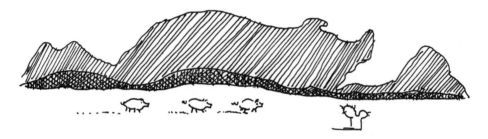

## WORLD'S TALLEST PIG

Marsha Swamp, who is only twelve and growing faster than you can read this, may be the tallest pig in the world. Marsha's parents claim that she is nine feet tall in her stocking feet. But no one knows for sure *how* tall Marsha is— she's never found a reason to stand up!

## WORLD'S SHORTEST PIG

Bo Bee, who even has a short name, is looked down upon as the shortest pig in the world. Bo is so short, he has to stand on the shoulders of four pigs to see the sun. He is so short, he has to jump *up* to wallow in the mud.

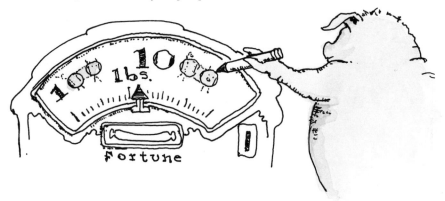

## WORLD'S SKINNIEST PIG

Butch O'Swinely, who stays slender by eating only twelve meals a day (not counting breakfast) is the world's skinniest pig. Butch is so skinny, he could fit into size 8000 hog swimming trunks—if anyone made them that small. Butch's secret for keeping his weight down? Tamper with the scale!

## WORLD'S BEST-DEVELOPED PIG

Porker Jarvis, who claims that on a clear day he can find where his biceps should be, is the world's best-developed pig. As a result of never moving more than six inches in any direction, Jarvis does not have an ounce of muscle or a single hard spot on his entire body. He is 850 pounds of solid flab. (And quite a show-off because of it!)

## WORLD'S MOST MUSCULAR PIG

Englebert Glut, who works out by lifting corn cobs to his mouth, is the world's most muscular pig. Glut has a total of 675 muscles in his body. They are all located in his snout!

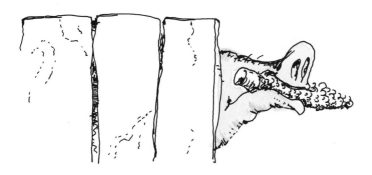

## WORLD'S WEAKEST PIG

Murray Hamm, who says that his most strenuous exercise is "trying to stay asleep," is the world's weakest pig. Hamm is so weak that he cannot raise his eyebrows without assistance. For this reason, he is the hero of millions of pigs far and wide (mostly wide).

## WORLD'S BEST PIG STUDENT

Homer deHogg, who brings an apple core to his teacher every day, is the world's best pig student. Homer's favorite class is Food Appreciation. "I have a real appetite for learning," he says. The studious Homer has cracked many a book. He doesn't read them — he only cracks them.

## WORLD'S WORST PIG STUDENT

Clete Bleat, who once tried to attend night school in the afternoon, may be the world's worst pig student. Clete is so bad in school, he still doesn't know how to spell the letter B. His classmates have voted him Most Likely to Remain a Pig for the Rest of His Life.

## WORLD'S BEST-EDUCATED PIG

The widely known and avoided Bertrand Snuffle is known as the world's best-educated pig. Snuffle got this reputation by once eating eighteen college diplomas in a single afternoon. Snuffle is so well-educated, he can get indigestion in six different languages.

## WORLD'S LARGEST PIG

Mike "Mountain" McPorkenbeans, who weighs himself in square miles instead of pounds, is the world's largest pig. McPorkenbeans is so large that no one dared refuse him when he insisted on being listed in this book for a second time!

## WORLD'S WEALTHIEST PIG

Harrison Hogg IV, whose ancestors made sure that the *Mayflower* was not a first-class ship, is the world's wealthiest pig. Hogg lives in a two-story, Colonial-style pig sty. Behind the sty, Hogg has his own mud pool with diving board and sun deck, and two mud courts on which he would play tennis if he hadn't eaten all the tennis balls.

It is rumored that in Colonial days, some of Paul Revere's pigs actually stepped in the antique silver pig trough from which Hogg now eats his slops. (Hogg's slops are flown in freshly spoiled from Paris, France, each week.)

Hogg is definitely a member of the upper crust. In fact, he actually *has* an upper crust, the result of never taking a bath.

Despite his family's many years in America, Hogg still takes an active interest in England. And he has adopted the British way of speaking. Instead of "oink, oink," Hogg says, "Hoink, hoink."

We interrupt *The Pigs' Book of World Records*
for the results of…

THE NATIONAL PIG AWARDS

# THE NATIONAL PIG AWARDS

The National Pig Awards for Meritorious Piggishness and Hoggishness Beyond the Call of Piggery are awarded each year to those pigs who demonstrate meritorious piggery or hoggery beyond the call of piggishness.

(This year, the banquet following the awards ceremony had to be canceled because of piggishness beyond the call of hoggishness, which resulted in all of the food being gobbled up *during* the awards ceremony. After the awards ceremony, the *awards* were also eaten!)

Here are this year's results . . .

FOR THE MOST GRACEFUL PIG:
No winner

FOR THE CLEANEST PIG:
No winner

FOR THE MOST ACTIVE PIG:
No winner

FOR THE MOST INTELLECTUAL PIG:
No winner

FOR THE MOST HONORED PIG:
No winner

# More Pig Records

## WORLD'S BEST CHEF

Chef Hardy Lard, whose Garbage Soufflé has been compared to the finest swill in Europe, is the world's best pig chef. Pigs who dine on Chef Lard's cuisine usually gobble up the silverware and the tablecloth in order to savor *every* divine morsel.

Why is Chef Lard's food so much better than that of other pig chefs? Says Lard: "My secret is *not* to sit in the food until just before I serve it."

## WORLD'S WORST CHEF

Chef Chomper Gumms, who says he learned all he knows about fine cuisine from lying in the mud, may be the world's worst pig chef. Chef Gumms once prepared a seventeen-course dinner for two pigs that was so bad it took them more than thirty seconds to eat it all. (Gumms left town in disgrace and has found suitable employment as a cook in a school cafeteria.)

## WORLD'S LONGEST SLEEPER

Eustace R. Boar, who once slept for 3 days, 17 hours, and 22 minutes, holds the pigs' world record for sleeping. Boar would have slept longer, but he wanted to get up in time for his afternoon nap!

## WORLD'S SHORTEST SLEEPER

Minnie Squeal, who believes that sleeping is good for you because it gives you a chance to rest, is the record holder for short sleeping. Poor Minnie can only nap for an hour at a time. Luckily, she manages to squeeze in at least twenty-four naps a day.

*Mechanical specifications—there is no clapper in bell, making alarm less annoying.

## WORLD'S MOST UNUSUAL SLEEPER

Barney Murk, who laughs a lot for no reason at all, may be the most unusual pig sleeper in the world. This is because Barney can sleep only while standing up. What makes this so unusual is that Barney *never* stands up when he's awake!

## WORLD'S MOST ANNOYING SLEEPER

Murphy LaPigg, who is also extremely annoying while awake, has been nominated by his friends as the world's most annoying sleeper. Murphy tosses and turns, spins and rolls over constantly while he sleeps. His friends find this annoying because he usually sleeps in the food trough, and all his moving about makes it difficult for them to eat around him!

## WORLD'S BEST DANCE TEAM

The team of Bacon & Leggs has had audiences rolling in the aisles (and in the dirt) for years with their marvelous tap dance routines. "The best hoofers on hooves" is how *Barnyard Variety* has described them. Their act is even more spectacular when you stop to consider how hard it is to make a tapping sound on mud.

## WORLD'S MOST UNUSUAL DREAM

Mary Swilly (rhymes with *silly*) has a most unusual recurring dream. Mary's dream is that her name appears in *The Pigs' Book of World Records*. In her unusual dream, Mary is listed in the book under the heading, "Most Unusual Dream." Her friends all think she's crazy.

## BEST HIGH JUMP BY A PIG

Cloven Barnes, who stays in top condition by lifting his weight every time he stands up, has broken every pigs' record for the high jump. Barnes's high jump record—¾ of an inch!

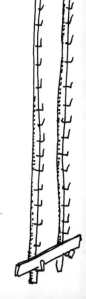

19

## WORLD'S WORST DANCE TEAM

The team of Bacon & Leggs, who let success go to their heads and each put on nearly eight hundred pounds since the paragraph on page 19 was written, are now the world's worst pig dance team. They can no longer raise their bellies off the ground in order to put on their tap shoes, and their pathetic attempts to polka instead of tap have disappointed audiences and set off earthquakes in several cities.

## FIRST PIG TO FLY CROSS-COUNTRY

Garland Glutton became the first pig to fly cross-country, when he flew in a 707 jet from a warehouse on Long Island to another warehouse in San Francisco. Unfortunately, Glutton wasn't aware of his exciting trip. He was a canned ham at the time.

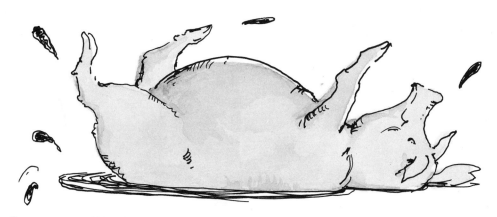

## WORLD'S BEST SWIMMER

Florence Pigwick, whose beautiful pig figure looks great in a twelve-piece bathing suit, is the world's best pig swimmer. Florence recently did the backstroke for 16 hours and 12 minutes without a stop. "Someday," she says, "if I can get out of this mud, I'm going to try my backstroke in water!"

## WORLD'S BEST MOUNTAIN CLIMBER

Simeon Snout, who admits that he's terrified of heights, depths, and whatever comes in between, astounded the climbing world by leaving his home and climbing to the top of Mount McMolehill in only seventeen days! (Snout's home is a good six inches from the top of Mount McMolehill.)

## WORLD'S FUNNIEST COMEDIAN

Henny Pigman, the barnyard comedian whose famous comedy line "Take my swine—please!" has had pigs laughing like monkeys, is the world's funniest pig. Pigman's classic baseball comedy routine— "Who Ate First, What Ate Second" —is so funny that audiences sometimes stop eating just to laugh at it. Pigman breaks up audiences by ending his act with the words, "Don't applaud—just throw garbage."

## BEST LONG JUMP BY A PIG

Cloven Barnes also holds the pigs' world record for the long jump. From a running start, he once leaped a distance of 1½ inches! (Unfortunately, the record was disallowed when it was learned that Barnes had received a push from a friend.)

## WORLD'S LARGEST PIG

Mike "Mountain" McPorkenbeans is still the largest pig in the world and is using his tremendous size to bully us into mentioning him more times than we really would have preferred.

FLASH! Stop the press! We couldn't wait for this book to end to bring you the results of THE PIGS' OPINION POLL!

How do pigs feel about the major issues of the day? The Pigs' Opinion Poll attempted to find out. More than three thousand pigs were questioned for this poll. Nearly thirty of them could hold up their heads long enough to respond. Here are the fascinating results...

QUESTION: DO YOU FEEL THAT ENOUGH MEASURES HAVE BEEN TAKEN TO COMBAT CRIME IN RURAL AND URBAN AREAS?

Don't Know.........................................15%
Not Sure .........................................20%
Please Repeat the Question ....................45%
Undecided ......................................40%

QUESTION: DO YOU FEEL THAT WE ARE MAKING PROGRESS IN FINDING WAYS TO PROTECT THE ENVIRONMENT?

What Did You Say? ............................70%
What Do Those Words Mean? ................30%
Could We Come Back to That One? .........35%
Undecided ......................................75%

QUESTION: ARE THINGS HARDER OR EASIER FOR YOU THAN THEY WERE FOR YOUR PARENTS?

Yes ...............................................55%
Maybe.............................................55%
Can't Remember My Parents...................55%
Can't Remember the Question .................55%

QUESTION: DO YOU THINK PIGS ARE DECISIVE ENOUGH?

Maybe.............................................60%
Perhaps ...........................................20%
Can't Decide......................................20%
Undecided........................................105%

# More Pig Records

## WORLD'S BEST FLOWER GARDEN BY A PIG

Barney Yard, who doesn't believe that fertilizer should be wasted on plants, has the most acclaimed flower garden of any pig in the world. In the colorful garden behind his swill pit, Barney has row after row of beautiful roses, gardenias, daffodils, violets, daisies, and chrysanthemums. How does Barney manage to keep so many fabulous flowers?

"My secret," he says, "is that I only eat one row a day."

## WORLD'S FASTEST LAWN MOWER

Knuckles Andwich, whose front lawn is so beautiful that pigs avoid it for miles around, keeps his grass neatly trimmed and holds the pigs' world record for fast lawn-cutting. "It takes me only about two hours to cut the grass," Andwich says proudly. "I could do it faster, but the weeds get caught in my teeth."

## WORLD'S BEST PIG DOCTOR

Dr. Piggy Pasteur, who has eaten medical textbooks from many of the nation's finest medical schools, worked in his lab for 22 years and astounded the medical world by discovering 566 new incurable diseases. Unfortunately, the next weekend, Dr. Pasteur came down with all of them!

## WORLD'S MOST BEAUTIFUL PIG STY

The world's most expensive and most beautiful pig sty belongs to the French interior desecrator Guy de Saint Glouton. Monsieur Glouton's sty is an eight-story edifice, each room decorated in a different classical period, with imported wallpapers, tiles, and furnishings from all over the globe. Unfortunately, no one has ever seen the inside of this magnificent palace. It smells too bad to go in!

Enlarged view of fly.

## WORLD'S UGLIEST PIG STY

Martin Gruckle's sty is located in the middle of a sludge pile, which means it's in the best of neighborhoods. But, despite this advantage, Gruckle has disgraced himself and angered his neighbors by keeping his sty spotlessly clean. According to his outraged neighbors, Gruckle's walls and floors have *less* than six inches of filth caked on them! A recent inspection of the premises turned up fewer than three thousand flying insects inside Gruckle's sty—certain grounds for eviction.

28

## WORLD'S LARGEST STAMP COLLECTOR

Benny Mudd has made the record books for being the world's largest pig stamp collector—even though his collection consists of only two stamps. Benny is the world's largest pig stamp collector because he weighs 950 pounds! (He's also the world's largest pig coin collector.)

## WORLD'S LARGEST INSECT COLLECTION

Roscoe "Fats" Slobbe has amazed the pig world with his ever-increasing insect collection. At last count, Roscoe had collected 3,500 ants and 2,300 flies. Unfortunately, they're all on his back!

## WORLD'S LARGEST SEA SHELL COLLECTION

Lucy Grovel takes real pride in showing friends her collection of more than 3,700 sea shells—all from polluted and filth-covered, condemned beaches. If you hold one of Lucy's sea shells up to your ear, you can hear Lake Erie!

## WORLD'S FINEST ART COLLECTION

Winkley Wharton Westerfield Wainright III, who is so refined he uses a lobster fork to clean the swill from his ears, has the finest collection of original paintings of any pig in the world. Wainright III (who prefers to be called III) owns paintings by such artists as Picasso, Monet, and Renoir. Which painting is his favorite?

"I really can't decide," he says. "Some days I like to sit on the Picasso. Other days I like to sit on the Monet or the Renoir."

## WORLD'S NICEST PIG

Mike "Mountain" McPorkenbeans is known everywhere you can possibly think of as the world's nicest pig. (He isn't really, but he *is* the world's largest pig, as you may already know, and if he'd also like to be known as the world's nicest pig, there isn't much we can do about it.)

## WORLD'S MOST-MENTIONED PIG IN A PIGS' RECORD BOOK

Guess who? We're really sorry, but you should see the size of him!

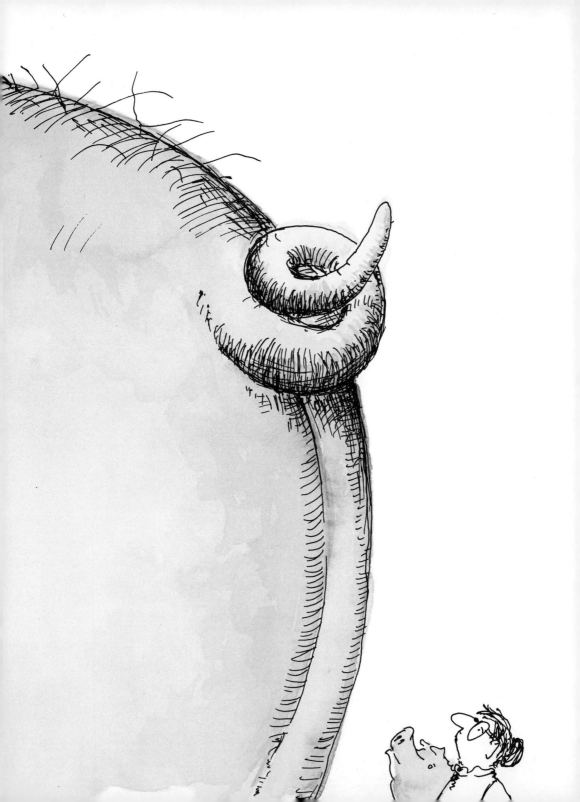

# **INDEX** to
## *The Pigs' Book of World Records*

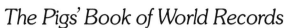

## F

Forget It: *See* pig

## G

Garden, flower, best by a pig: *See* best
Glutton: *See* pig

## H

Having a Good Time, Wish You Were Here:
*See* postcard
Heaviest Pig: *See* pig, heaviest

## I

I am not finding anything in this index: *See* pig
Index, not anything I am finding in it: *See* I

## L

Largest Art Collection, by a pig: *See* pig
Largest Flower Garden, by a pig: *See* your eye doctor
Largest Pig: *See* McPorkenbeans (if you must)

## M

Most Athletic Pig: *See* athletic, pig, most
Most Foolish: *See* reader of this index
Mountain Climber, best: *See* pig, climber, mountain, best

## P

Prettiest: *See* a different book
Pretty Good Mountain Climber: *See* pig

## R

Reasonably Good Mountain Climber: *See* pretty good
mountain climber

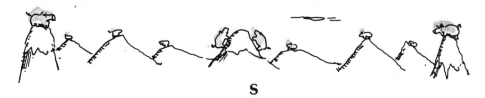

## S

Shortest: *See* shrtst
Sleeper, best: *See* sleeper, best pig
Sleeper, worst: *See* pig
Smartest Pig: *See* stupid
Strongest: *See* pig, athletic, most
Sty, most beautiful: *See* Hoggingham Palace
Swimmer, best: *See* best swimmer

## T

Tallest: *See* shortest
The Art Collection, pig, best by a: *See* art
The Most Athletic Pig: *See* pig, athletic, most, the
The Silliest: *See* index

## U

Ugliest Pig: *See* 1,000-way tie for first place

## W

Weakest Pig, world, in the: *See* pig
Wealthiest, world, the, in, pig: *See* spots before your eyes

## Z

Ze End to this Index: *See* pig

Before we begin the next book, we have this important

## ANNOUNCEMENT

The doctor will be available this afternoon. Those pigs who are not suffering from indigestion, heartburn, overweight, lice, fleas, and infection due to unclean habits *must* see the doctor to find out what they are doing wrong.

GURGLE BLOAT BELCH BLUB

38

# BOOK 2
# THE WORLD'S WORST PIG JOKE BOOK!

With an introduction
by Barney Yard-Odor

Come on, you pigs—no walking here!
Let's try to keep this book NEAT!

39

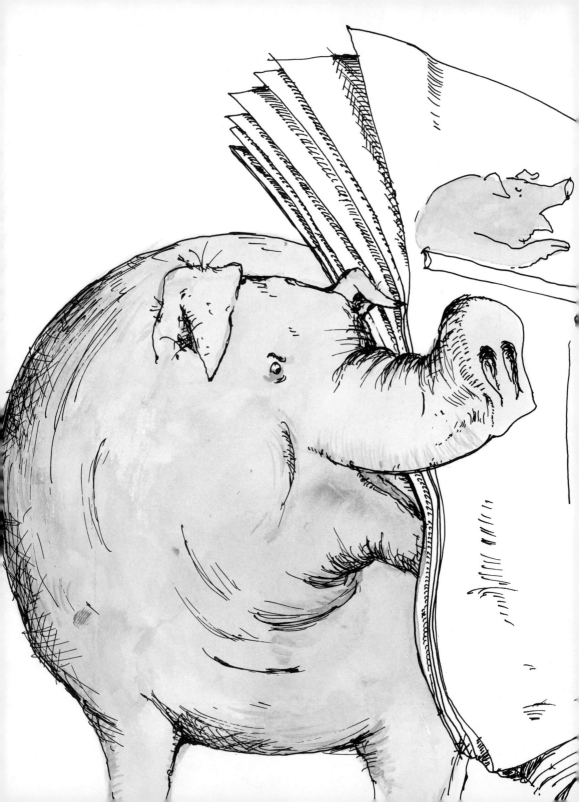

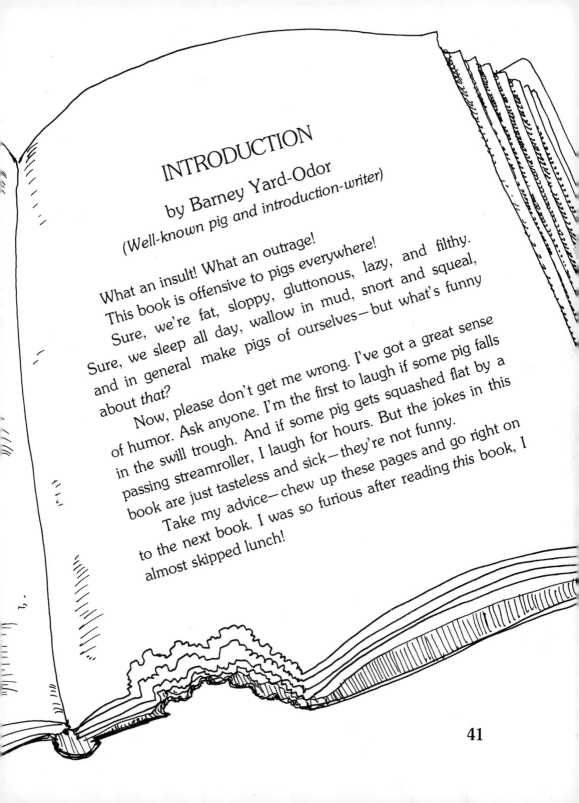

# INTRODUCTION

by Barney Yard-Odor

*(Well-known pig and introduction-writer)*

What an insult! What an outrage! This book is offensive to pigs everywhere! Sure, we're fat, sloppy, gluttonous, lazy, and filthy. Sure, we sleep all day, wallow in mud, snort and squeal, and in general make pigs of ourselves—but what's funny about that?

Now, please don't get me wrong. I've got a great sense of humor. Ask anyone. I'm the first to laugh if some pig falls in the swill trough. And if some pig gets squashed flat by a passing streamroller, I laugh for hours. But the jokes in this book are just tasteless and sick—they're not funny.

Take my advice—chew up these pages and go right on to the next book. I was so furious after reading this book, I almost skipped lunch!

41

# The World's Worst Pig Jokes

Q: What do you call a champion pig who weighs in at 580 pounds?
A: Slim.

Q: What's the best way to call a pig?
A: Long distance.

Q: What is the pigs' favorite play?
A: HAMlet.

Q: What do you call a twenty-two-room, four-story mansion lived in by a pig?
A: A pig sty.

Q: How do the pigs kick off their Super Bowl?
A: From the 40-lard line.

Q: What do you call a pig who fights with a killer shark?
A: Dummy.

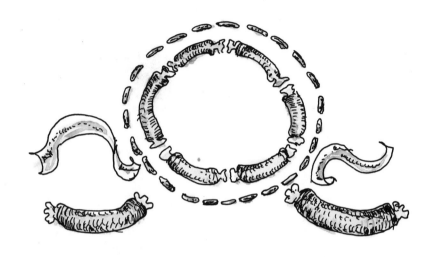

Q: What do you call two pigs who fight with a killer shark?
A: Sausage.

Q: Why is a pig like a fish?
A: They both have gills except for the pig.

Q: What do you call a pig with an inch-thick crust of year-old dirt all over his body?
A: Clean.

Q: Who is the pigs' favorite author?
A: Jovial Bob Swine.

Q: Why did the pig get a traffic ticket?
A: He didn't see the No Porking sign.

We interrupt the *World's Worst Pig Joke Book* for this important

## ACTING LESSON!

The great pig actor, Hammond Bacon-on-the-Syde, demonstrates the dramatic facial expressions that have made his reputation:

SURPRISE　　　　SADNESS

JOY　　　　GRIEF

FEAR　　　　HUNGER

# More Pig Jokes

Q: How can you tell a pig from a disgusting pile of mud?
A: You usually can't.

Q: What did the pig say when given an award as the world's most cultured and well-spoken pig?
A: Oink.

Q: What do you call karate moves made by a pig?
A: Pork chops.

Q: What do you call an archaeological expedition made by important pig scientists?
A: A bigwig pig dig.

Nautical note: A—water line
B—pig line

Q: What do you call a pig who is carried across a river in a small boat?
A: A rowed hog.

Q: What happened when the pig climbed an evergreen tree?
A: He became a porkupine.

Q: Where do the rich pigs live in New York City?
A: On Pork Avenue.

Q: How do you treat a pig who has skinned his knee?
A: You apply an oinkment.

Q: What do you call a clumsy pig fire-eater in the circus?
A: Smoked ham.

Q: How can you tell a pig from a horse?
A: The pig is the one that doesn't look like a horse.

Q: What do you call a seven-course dinner served by the world's finest pig chef?

A: Garbage.

Q: Why did the bank robbers refuse to take a pig into their gang?
A: They were afraid he might squeal.

Q: Why did the pig run headfirst into a brick wall?
A: Because he was a crashing boar.

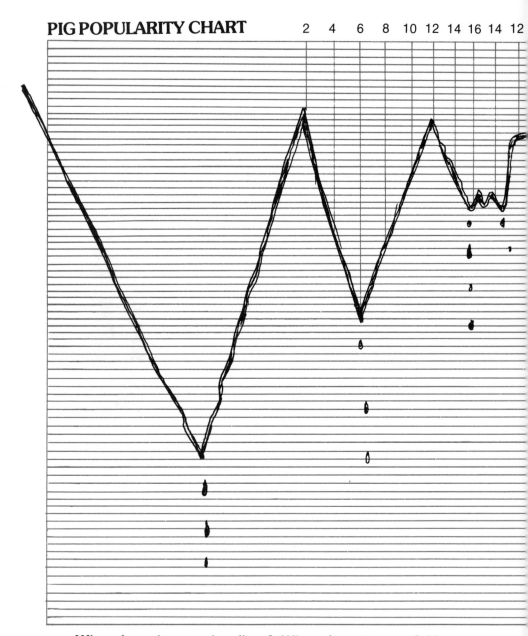

# PIG POPULARITY CHART

2  4  6  8  10 12 14 16 14 12

What does this graph tell us? What does it mean? No one around here has the foggiest!

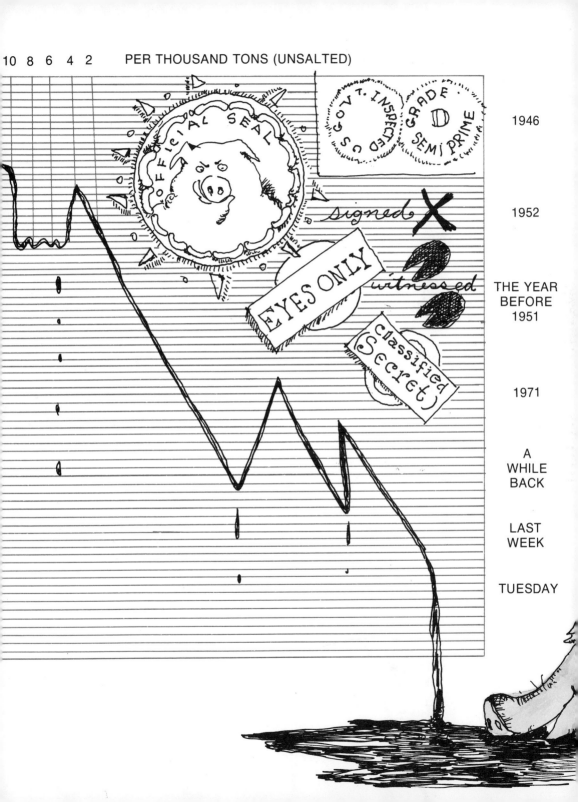

Before we begin the next book,
we have this important

## ANNOUNCEMENT!

The Rose Bush Squashing Party scheduled for tonight
has been canceled due to the thoughtlessness of a few pigs
who squashed the rose bushes this morning. The Gardenia
Stomping Get-Together will be held as scheduled.

# BOOK 3

# THE JOY OF SWILL!
## A Cookbook for Pigs

by Park R. Porker, Parker Porker,
Porker Parker, and Pork R. Parker

Copy of engraving of Pilgrim Pig at Thanksgiving dinner.

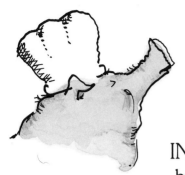

# INTRODUCTION
## by Park R. Porker

My colleagues and myself found it impossible to agree on which recipes to include in this book. We wrestled with the problem and we wrestled with each other. We pushed each other around in the mud, sat on each other, and threw each other headfirst into the slops trough—but all of these efforts failed to help us reach any decisions. Finally, we decided to toss in whatever we could and go have supper.

There is a lesson here somewhere, and I'm sure you'll find out what it is if you try these recipes.

## ADDITIONAL NOTE

## by Pork R. Parker

Some of these dishes actually made me sick, but I was outvoted.

# GUIDE TO PIG MEASUREMENTS

For preparing these recipes, it will often be necessary to translate human measurements into pig measurements. Use this handy guide:

| Human Measurements | | Pig Measurements |
| --- | --- | --- |
| 1 teaspoon | = | 1 wheelbarrow |
| 1 tablespoon | = | 2 vats |
| 1 cup | = | 3 troughs |
| 1 pint | = | 2 vats, 2 troughs, 1 teaspoon |
| 1 quart | = | 1 Olympic-size swimming pool |
| 1 gallon | = | 1 lake |
| 1 ounce | = | 4 tons |
| 8 ounces | = | 6 vats, 4 troughs, and just a dash |
| 1 pound | = | The city of Detroit |

# AND NOW...THE RECIPES

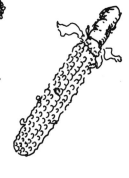

## CORN COBS À LA CORN COBS

*Ingredients:*

**corn cobs
cobs of corn
corn on the cob (without the
     corn)
assorted cobs
variety of corn cobs (whole)
several de-vegetabled corn
     cobs
pinch corn cob**

Place the corn cobs in a large mixing bowl. Slowly add the cobs of corn. Stir gently, adding corn on the cob (making sure the corn has been removed).

On a separate plate, combine the assorted cobs, the variety of corn cobs (whole), and several de-vegetabled corn cobs. Allow both mixtures to set for a few seconds and then combine the corn cobs / cobs of corn / corn on the cob mixture with the assorted cobs / variety of corn cobs / de-vegetabled corn cobs mixture.

When completely combined, season with a pinch of corn cob.

# FILLET OF SLOPS IN CREAM SAUCE

*Ingredients:*

**4 quarts slops**
**sour milk (sour buttermilk**
**can be substituted if you**
**like a lot of lumpy stuff**
**in your food)**

To fillet the slops, simply remove all the bones with your snout. The bones can be eaten as a marvelous side dish. Add the sour milk slowly, allowing the slops to curdle in the sun. If you cannot stand the odor, perhaps your milk isn't quite sour enough.

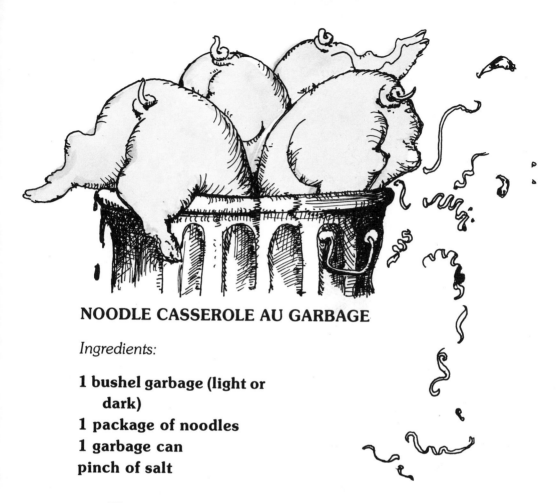

## NOODLE CASSEROLE AU GARBAGE

*Ingredients:*

**1 bushel garbage (light or
    dark)**
**1 package of noodles**
**1 garbage can**
**pinch of salt**

This recipe tastes best with green noodles. If your noodles aren't green, let them sit around until they turn green. Add the garbage to the noodles and allow to simmer in the garbage can. When the mixture attracts enough flies to cover top, mixture has simmered long enough. If there is mud in the garbage can, you probably won't need the pinch of salt.

Serves: as many as can squeeze their heads into the garbage can.

## SLOPS SALAD "BLOAT"

*Ingredients:*

**orange rinds
apple cores
pineapple skins
banana peels
grass and weeds (to taste)
slops
1 maraschino cherry**

The secret to this salad is the quality of the grass and weeds you use. If your grass and weeds are covered with fleas, mites, ticks, chiggers, and other insects and insect larvae, you will have a tastier salad. Be sure to add enough slops to make your stomach bloat up like a balloon *before* you have finished eating.

## COMBAT BOOT IN SNAIL SAUCE

*Ingredients:*

**1 bullwhip**
**1 snail**
**1 boot**

Whip the snail until it becomes sauce. Add the boot. Bake the boot at 350°(unless someone is wearing it).

While you have the bullwhip handy, you might want to make a whipped cream topping for your boot. (For heavy cream, whip the cow harder than usual.)

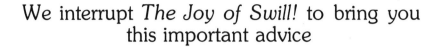

We interrupt *The Joy of Swill!* to bring you this important advice

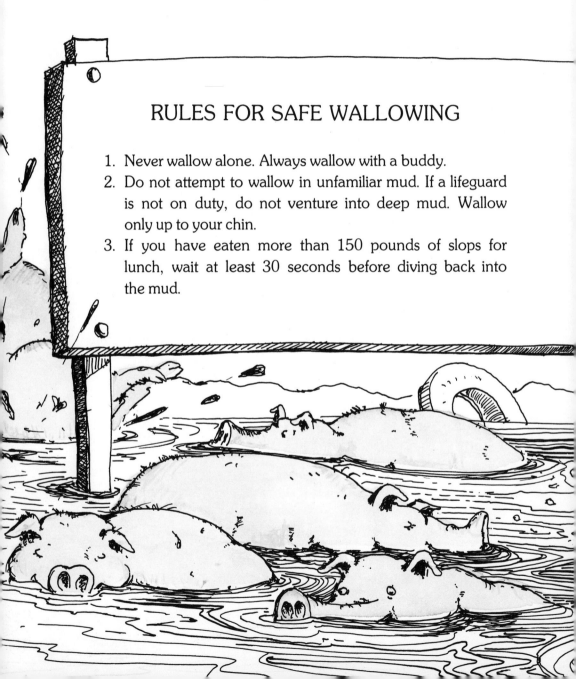

## RULES FOR SAFE WALLOWING

1. Never wallow alone. Always wallow with a buddy.
2. Do not attempt to wallow in unfamiliar mud. If a lifeguard is not on duty, do not venture into deep mud. Wallow only up to your chin.
3. If you have eaten more than 150 pounds of slops for lunch, wait at least 30 seconds before diving back into the mud.

4. Look before you dive. Make sure there is a crowd around. You don't want to jump in if you can't splash mud on others.
5. Keep your mouth closed and try not to swallow mud. If you swallow too much mud, it will ruin your appetite for mealtime.
6. Never shower before entering the mud. Why spoil a perfectly filthy mud pile for others?

and now, back to the recipes . . .

Cooked by J.B. SWINE
Canned by P.LIPPIG
MARCH ng

## HOOF AND MOUTH DISEASE CHOWDER

This chowder is made very rarely because it's too disgusting to describe. We won't go into detail here, but if there's an outbreak of hoof and mouth disease in your area, congratulations — and *bon appétit!*

## JELL-O MOLD

*Ingredients:*

**1 package very old Jell-O**

It's easier than you think to grow a delicious mold on Jell-O. You just have to wait long enough, making sure to keep your package of Jell-O damp and warm. Before you know it, that taste-tempting mold will grow right before your delighted eyes.

For summertime, try growing a cool green mold in a lime Jell-O package. Or how about a tart and tasty blue mold on raspberry Jell-O for a colorful fall dish? Sprinkle with mildew and bite right into the package. It's the perfect furry dessert!

## SLIGHTLY ILL BIRD BARBECUE

*Ingredients:*

**1 slightly ill bird**
**1 sunny day**

Your bird will not taste good unless properly prepared.
To prepare bird properly, hold it up to the sun.

When bird is rare or medium rare (or if it starts to feel
warm), remove it from the sun and eat.

If bird flies away, perhaps it was not ill enough.

## FILTH DISH

*Ingredients:*

**assorted filth**
**1 dish (unclean, if possible)**

This popular dessert dish will not succeed unless you remember one essential rule: You must stand in the filth for at least twenty minutes before serving the dish. Never, never wash first. Some pigs like to place a vanilla ice cream carton on top of the filth for Filth à la Mode.

(If you are using Instant Filth, be sure to follow the instructions and add enough muddy water.)

Additional copies of *The Joy of Swill!* will be destroyed upon request. Write to: Park R. Porker, Parker Porker, or Porker Parker. Please do not write to Pork R. Parker. He's feeling a little queasy and had to go lie down.

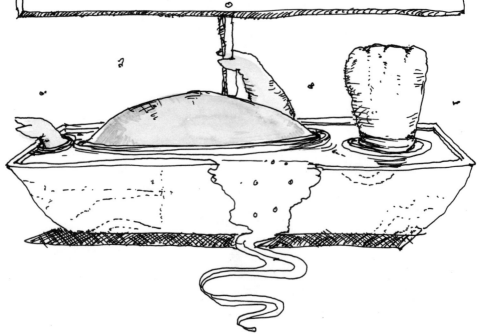

While all of you pigs are waiting for the next book to begin, why not take a few seconds out to see how you rate on...

## THE PIGS' DATING TEST

All pigs, as they grow into swinehood, will go out on dates. What kind of breeding will *you* show on a date? Will you be mature, thoughtful, sophisticated, and act like a real swine? Or will your hammy manners and barnyard behavior force your date to wish that he or she was home by the swill bucket—alone? Choose the right answer for each question to determine what kind of pig you will be on a date.

1. Before a big dance, your date brings you a corsage. You:

   (a) thank him kindly and put it on
   (b) thank him kindly and eat it
   (c) wait until you get to the dance to eat it

Correct Answer: Thank him kindly, unwrap the flowers, eat half of them immediately, and offer the other half to your date. He probably will not have eaten for thirty seconds or so, and will be grateful for the snack.

71

2. You are walking to the dance and come upon a large mud puddle. You:

  (a) wait at the edge and allow your date to carry you over the puddle
  (b) walk around the puddle
  (c) dive into the puddle and wallow

Correct Answer: Allow your date to wallow first, then share the mud for as long as it takes to get truly filthy. No one should ever arrive clean to a dance—even if it's a first date.

3. You arrive at the dance and the music starts. You should:

  (a) step out on the floor and start dancing
  (b) excuse yourself to go make sure your hair is in disarray
  (c) eat all the refreshments off the refreshment table and then dance

Correct Answer: By all means, eat all of the refreshments first! You can always dance later. But if you wait till five minutes after the dance begins, there won't be a scrap of food left!

4. A group of eight or ten pigs has gathered in a corner and is laughing and talking instead of dancing. You should:

   (a) be sociable and join them
   (b) quietly ask your date to dance
   (c) smear mud on your face so everyone will ask where you got such a lovely tan

Correct Answer: While everyone's talking, go back to the refreshment stand. There might be a few scraps that were missed.

5. Your date walks you back to your sty and tries to kiss you. You should:

   (a) pour a bucket of swill over his head
   (b) kiss him
   (c) suggest that you're not that kind of pig

Correct Answer: Pour a bucket of swill over his head. That's really what he's interested in. He just asked for the kiss to be polite.

Before we begin the next book,
we have this important

## ANNOUNCEMENT

The following books are missing from the pigs' library:

*Moby Pig*
*Hoggleberry Finn*
*The Great Fatsby*
*The Lardy Boys Mystery Adventures*

Will the pig who took these volumes please return them? The librarian needs these books to sit on, since she outgrew her chair last week.

# BOOK 4

# THE PIGS' BOOK OF LISTS

With an introduction
by Olive R. Lardy

oink

# INTRODUCTION
## by Olive R. Lardy
### *(Well-known author and pig)*

At last! A collection of useless and uninformative facts about us pigs — collected in convenient and easy-to-forget lists!

Everyone enjoys reading lists. So everyone should enjoy this book because that's all it is.

In closing, I would like to list the reasons why I'm sure you will enjoy the lists in this book:

1. Each one is numbered so you don't get too confused.
2.
3.
4.
5. I can't think of any other reasons.
6.
7.
8.

# The Pigs' Book of Lists

## FIVE MOST POPULAR PIG TRACK AND FIELD EVENTS

1. High hurdle avoiding
2. 100-yard crawl
3. The low jump
4. Marathon sleeping relay
5. Javelin catching

## SIX QUALITIES PIGS LOOK FOR IN A MATE

1. Rudeness
2. Laziness
3. Sloppiness
4. Fatness
5. Good sense of humor
6. Good dancer

## SIX QUALITIES PIGS TRY TO AVOID IN A MATE

1. Won't share slops
2. Not a good provider
3. Won't share swill
4. Gobbles up others' food
5. Won't share garbage
6. Doesn't snore

## THREE LITTLE-KNOWN PIGS WHO WISH TO REMAIN LITTLE KNOWN

1. Name withheld by request
2. Name withheld by request
3. Name withheld by request

## FOUR NICKNAMES THAT HAVE NEVER BEEN GIVEN TO PIGS

1. "Speedy"
2. "Professor"
3. "Beanpole"
4. "Cuddles"

## FIVE INVENTIONS OF THE FUTURE THAT PIGS WOULD LIKE TO SEE

1. Instant mud
2. Air-conditioned slops trough
3. Edible sun visors
4. Portable lawn chair that can hold 950 pounds
5. Swill-on-a-stick

## FIVE MOST POPULAR PIG VACATION SPOTS

1. The north forty
2. The south forty
3. Behind the hayloft
4. Under the slops trough
5. Miami Beach

## FIVE REASONS WHY PIGS DON'T GO TO SCHOOL

1. Desks are too high
2. Lockers are poorly constructed, swill leaks out
3. Showers are required after gym class
4. Oinking is not allowed in the halls
5. Textbooks taste dry

## TEN WAYS PIGS ENJOY EATING EGGS

1. Whole in shell
2. Whole in shell covered with dirt
3. Whole in chicken
4. Just the whites with yolk smeared on face
5. Smeared on face with shell ground into ears
6. Scrambled in year-old grease
7. Scrambled after swallowed
8. Sunny side up, then sat on for an hour
9. Sunny side up, then smeared on face
10. Cheese and mushroom omelette

We interrupt *The Pigs' Book of Lists* for this

## HISTORIC SPEECH!

Here is the complete text of a speech delivered by Ulysses S. Grunt, former president of the Hog Haranguers Bureau, and today, chairman of the board of Pigs for a Noisier America:

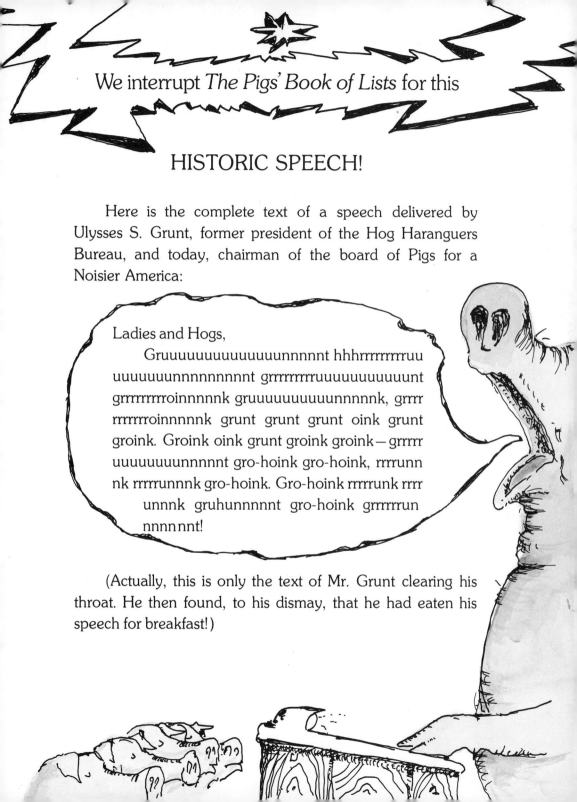

Ladies and Hogs,

Gruuuuuuuuuuuuuuunnnnnt hhhrrrrrrrruu uuuuuuunnnnnnnnnt grrrrrrrruuuuuuuuuuunt grrrrrrrroinnnnnk gruuuuuuuuuunnnnnk, grrrr rrrrrroinnnnnk grunt grunt grunt oink grunt groink. Groink oink grunt groink groink — grrrrr uuuuuuuunnnnnt gro-hoink gro-hoink, rrrrunn nk rrrrunnnk gro-hoink. Gro-hoink rrrrrunk rrrr unnnk gruhunnnnnt gro-hoink grrrrrun nnnnnnt!

(Actually, this is only the text of Mr. Grunt clearing his throat. He then found, to his dismay, that he had eaten his speech for breakfast!)

## TEN MOST COMMON PIG ILLNESSES AND DISORDERS

1. Indigestion
2. Upset stomach
3. Heartburn
4. Upset stomach and heartburn
5. Another upset stomach
6. Queasiness around the stomach area with a touch of heartburn
7. Nausea, possibly due to indigestion
8. Nausea, possibly due to reading this list
9. Strained stomach muscles (usually accompanied by an upset stomach)
10. Lack of energy due to hunger

## FIVE MOST POPULAR CURES FOR PIG ILLNESSES AND DISORDERS

1. Eat more
2. Take larger bites
3. Eat larger items
4. Drink more liquids
5. Drink more solids

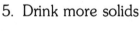

## THREE FAMOUS COMPOSERS WHO WERE NOT PIGS

1. Mozart
2. Chopin
3. Bach

## THREE PIGS WHO WERE NOT COMPOSERS

1. Frumpy Messer
2. Lump R. Chowder, Jr.
3. Porkbone Malone

## FIVE CITIES IN THE U.S. THAT HAVE NO PIGS

1. Allbright, New Mexico
2. Marvelous, Indiana
3. Swell City, South Carolina
4. Bestluckville, Alabama
5. Zowie, Ohio

## FIVE CLEANEST CITIES IN THE U.S.

1. Allbright, New Mexico
2. Marvelous, Indiana
3. Swell City, South Carolina
4. Bestluckville, Alabama
5. Zowie, Ohio

## TWO AUTHORS WHO COULD HAVE BEEN PIGS BUT WEREN'T

1. Sir Francis Bacon
2. Ring Lardner

## FOUR AUTHORS WHO COULD HAVE BEEN PIGS AND WERE

1. John Swinebeck
2. Herman Smellville
3. F. Scott Fatsgerald
4. Edgar Allan Pork

## SEVEN SENTENCES THAT ARE EXTREMELY OFFENSIVE TO PIGS

1. "Your room looks like a pig sty!"
2. "He's bringing home the bacon!"
3. "Don't be a road hog!"
4. "He's always been a ham actor!"
5. "That's solid pig-iron construction!"
6. "Let's toss around the old pigskin!"
7. "I'll have a BLT on toast!"

## FIVE MAJOR UNIVERSITIES THAT WILL NOT ENROLL PIGS

1. Harvard
2. Yale
3. Princeton
4. UCLA
5. University of Michigan (unless on a football scholarship)

## THREE UNIVERSITIES THAT WILL ENROLL PIGS

1. Armour Star Junior College and Packing Plant
2. Oscar Mayer Business University and Bologna Factory
3. Swift & Co. Finishing School

## TWO MOST POPULAR GAMES PLAYED BY YOUNG PIGS

1. Hide and Go Sleep
2. Pin the Tail on the Mud

# THREE MOST POPULAR PIG FOOTBALL CHEERS

1. "Oiiiiiiink Oiiiiiiink! Grunt Grunt Grunt!" (repeat)
2. "Groink groink groink? Groink groink groink! Groink groink groink? Groink groink groink! Go team!"
3. "Give me a G!"
   "G!"
   "Give me an R!"
   "R!"
   "Give me an O!"
   "O!"
   "Give me an I!"
   "I!"
   "Give me an N!"
   "N!"
   "Give me a K!"
   "K!"
   "What have you got?"
   "GROINK!"

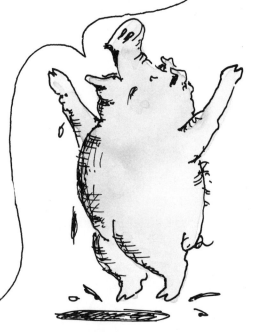

## THREE MOST COMMON COMPLAINTS PARENT PIGS HAVE ABOUT THEIR PIGLETS

1. "Why can't you stay dirty like everyone else?"
2. "Why do you have to keep your room so neat?"
3. "Eat five more desserts or you can't leave the table!"

# A Timeline of Pig History

From the primitive pigs of prehistoric days to the primitive pigs of today.

**B.C.**

*10,000*
Prehistoric pigs have not fully developed. Many still walk on two legs. Some early pig species still have wings. People believe them to be large pink sparrows. Confusion reigns.

Art historical note: These are actual reproductions of pig cave painting.

*8000*
Stone Age pigs attempt to wallow in stone. Receive severe cuts and bruises.

## 6300

Invention of the wheel astounds the world, changes life forever for humans. Pigs believe it to be a passing fad. Continue to use square roller skates.

## 4500

Early pig scientist combines water and dirt. Believes he has invented root beer. His soft drink is a failure since bottles and cans are still made out of stone, too heavy to carry home from supermarket.

## 3000

No major accomplishments by pigs in the past 1,500 years. This begins a trend that continues to this day.

## 2000

Attila the Hogg invades Poland. Discovers there is no one there yet. Decides to take a nap.

## 1500

Foolhardy Egyptian pig attempts to put out Great Pyramid fire by leaping onto the flames. Becomes the first baked ham. Egyptians go crazy looking for pineapple rings to put on top.

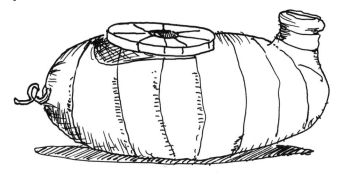

## 1000

Pig scientist wallows in mud for first time. Believes he has discovered a shorter route to India. Is asked to hoof it out of town at his earliest convenience.

## 500

Tribe of pigs adopts habit of wallowing head-down in mud. Soon becomes known as The Lost Tribe of Pigs.

# A.D.

*150*

Great-great-grandson of Attila the Hogg invades France in August. Finds everyone is away on vacation. Decides to take a nap.

*255*

Marco Piggo discovers way to turn old food into garbage. Garbage no longer must be imported from China. Piggo, however, travels to China to bring back necessary spices— mildew, rust, maggots, and vanilla.

*1100*

The Dark Ages. Pigs use flashlights to see what filth they're groveling in.

### 1220
Virginia Hamm becomes first pig to use the phrase, "Oink, oink." Phrase catches on all over the world, replacing previously popular pig saying, "Indubitably."

### 1492
Unknown pig explorer, Anonymous Pig, decides to stay home, since no one knows him anyway. Discovers a shorter route to his swill trough.

### 1620
Pigs sail on *Mayflower*. Are first to deface Plymouth Rock. American Indian pigs show the new arrivals how to eat corn cobs.

### 1776
Pigs fight during Revolutionary War. They fight over mud piles and swill troughs. Have no idea that there's a war going on.

## 1778

Pork Revere, noted pig patriot, wallows on his back in middle of road near Lexington and Concord in attempt to keep British soldiers from passing. Doesn't realize that soldiers already passed two years earlier!

## 1790

Pig philosopher Emmanuel Snout writes the immortal words, "I eat—therefore I am." No one can figure out what in blazes he's talking about! But for years to come, philosophical pigs eat up his books.

## 1849

"Garbage! Garbage!" is the excited cry from covered wagons heading west, as '49er pigs head for the Great California Garbage Rush. Disappointed pigs soon discover that California offers gold—not garbage—and most return home in disgust.

### 1862

Taylor Ham, grandson of a pig once kicked by Thomas Jefferson, decides to run for President of the United States. He fails to win much support. Ham's political ambitions end when he is eaten by a family of five on Christmas Eve.

### 1888

Marconi Piglioni invents the radio. Eats it for lunch.

### 1965

Neil Hamstrung becomes the first pig in space. No one knows how he got up there. There are no plans to bring him back.

### 1980

*The Pigs' Book of World Records* is published. Humans ignore it completely. Pigs find it "good eating once you chew through the cover."

# No Loitering!

This book is over. All pigs are asked to leave the premises quickly and quietly. Any pigs who ignore this notice will be forced to join the Clean-Up Committee, which will be working for several hours to clean up the mess you've made of the rest of this book!

# Some Other Books on This Topic You Probably Won't Enjoy

The Pigs' Book of Pigs
The Runners' Guide to Pigs
The Pigs' Guide to Pigs
The Pigs' Guide to Guides on Pigs
Pigs on Pigs
Pigs Look at Pigs—and Vice Versa
French for Pigs
The Pigs' Guide to Failure
100 Pigs—and How to Count Them
More Than 100 Pigs—and How to Avoid Counting Them
Fewer Than 100 Pigs but More Than 60
Pigs: Tragedy or Disaster?
The Pigs' Guide to Other Pigs' Books You Probaby Won't
    Enjoy

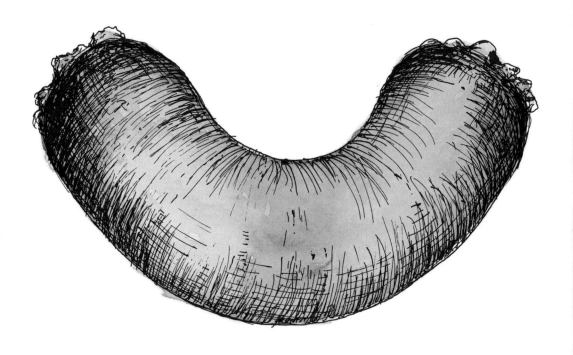

95

**Jovial Bob Stine** is the editor of *Bananas*, the popular monthly humor magazine for teenagers, and the clean, neat author of *How To Be Funny* and *The Absurdly Silly Encyclopedia and Fly Swatter*. He was born in Columbus, Ohio, and now lives in New York City with his wife, Jane.

**Peter Lippman** has illustrated many children's books by other authors and several he has written himself, including *New at the Zoo, Peter Lippman's One and Only Wacky Wordbook*, and *I Was Very Shy*. A native New Yorker, he lives part of the time in New York and part in the Catskill Mountains. One of his best friends raises pigs.